Family Story Collection

Hard Work
Leads to Success

Stories About Teamwork and Determination

Book Twelve

Printed in China
First Edition
1 3 5 7 9 10 8 6 4 2

ISBN 0-7868-3536-2

For more Disney Press fun, visit www.disneybooks.com

Book Twelve

———— ⨎ ————

Hard Work
Leads to Success

———— ⨎ ————

STORIES ABOUT TEAMWORK AND DETERMINATION

Introduction

When children are given everything they ask for, they miss out on a crucial phase of their development—experiencing the link between work and reward. As they grow older, things will not come as easily and they may resent having to work hard. Success is often the natural outcome of hard work, but hard work can be a reward in its own right.

In "An Unlikely Pair," Kuzco is used to being waited on. However, he learns that hard work is essential, and the reward he receives for his efforts cannot be greater—his own life. Meanwhile, Milo, in "Never Say Never," has a dream to find the lost city of Atlantis. No one believes it is possible. But finally, his hard work pays off, and Milo is able to pursue his dream to the ends of the earth—and the bottom of the sea.

An Unlikely Pair

from *The Emperor's New Groove*

Working together is the only way to work.

Pacha, the peasant, had been leading the emperor-turned-llama Kuzco back to the city where Kuzco lived when, all of a sudden, the bridge they were crossing collapsed and Pacha fell through! Now he was hanging on for dear life.

"Kuzco!" cried Pacha, "help me!"

Pacha twisted in the ropes and tried to look for Kuzco.

"No, I don't think I will," Kuzco said coldly.

Kuzco could see the city from where he stood. He could find his way home on his own now. He had no need for the peasant who had helped him.

"Buh-bye," said Kuzco.

He turned to walk away when . . . the bridge gave way beneath him, too! He was dangling by the ropes, just like Pacha.

"Are you okay?" asked a genuinely concerned Pacha.

"Yeah, I think I'm all right," replied the dazed Kuzco.

"Good," Pacha said, as he punched Kuzco square in the jaw.

Of course, Pacha had every reason to be angry, but it really wasn't an ideal time for a fistfight. Still, the two punched and kicked, and soon they both lost hold of the ropes. Down they fell, until they got wedged in a narrow crevice. They were still high above the river.

Hungry alligators snapped and circled in the water below. There was no more time for arguing.

"Now, we're gonna have to work together to get out of this, so follow my lead," said Pacha.

Pacha was used to teamwork. Kuzco was used to people working *for* him, not *with* him. But Kuzco had no choice. If he didn't learn to cooperate fast, they would both be alligator food.

Pacha showed him what to do. The two pushed their backs together, and slowly worked their way up the crevice.

"Look! We're moving!" cried Kuzco, surprised that the plan was actually working.

As they neared the top, Pacha noticed a rope from the bridge hanging down nearby. If only he could reach it, they could pull themselves up to the ledge.

"You're gonna have to trust me," Pacha told Kuzco.

Kuzco pushed Pacha up toward the rope with all his might. Pacha reached it! And

the two were able to get themselves up onto the ledge to safety.

They lay there for a moment, safe but stunned. Suddenly, the ledge beneath Pacha began to crumble. Just in the nick of time, Kuzco caught Pacha's shirt in his teeth and pulled him to solid ground.

Luckily for both of them, Kuzco's crash

course in teamwork was a success. He was beginning to see that sometimes the only way to work was to work together.

Never Say Never

from *Atlantis: The Lost Empire*

Never give up on your dreams.

Every free moment, Milo Thatch studied and researched dusty old books at his desk at the museum where he worked, in order to fulfill his lifelong dream—finding the lost city of Atlantis.

He was trying to figure out the clues in a book that described something called *The Shepherd's Journal*. It was supposed to contain a map of Atlantis. And after many months, he had a breakthrough.

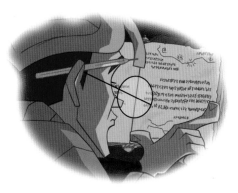

Milo practiced a speech explaining his discovery. "After comparing the text to the runes on the Viking shield, I found that one of the letters had been mistranslated," he said. "By changing this letter and inserting the correct one, we find that the key to Atlantis lies not in Ireland, but in Iceland!"

Milo tried to convince the museum board members to listen to his new theory. But they thought he was crazy for trying to find a place that probably didn't even exist. They began running away whenever they saw him, to keep from having to listen to him talk about Atlantis.

But Milo never let their doubts sway him. He was sure that Atlantis was out there somewhere. He only needed the chance to prove it.

One day, a wealthy man named Preston Whitmore summoned Milo to his mansion. Milo wasn't sure what the man wanted until Whitmore pulled out a distinctive-looking book. Milo gasped. It was *The Shepherd's Journal!*

It was just what Milo needed to figure out how to reach Atlantis. But it wouldn't do him much good on dry land. He needed to find a way to put the map to use.

"I will find Atlantis," he cried excitedly, "if I have to rent a rowboat!"

Whitmore leaned closer.

"Congratulations, Milo," he said. "This is exactly what I wanted to hear. But forget the rowboat, son. We'll travel in style!"

Milo gasped as he realized what this meant. Whitmore wanted to fund Milo's expedition to find Atlantis. And he wanted Milo to guide it! Before he knew it, Milo was standing on the deck of an enormous, state-of-the-art submarine. A full crew would help him search for the lost city.

Milo could hardly believe it. After all the dreams, all the studying, all the hard work and disappointments, his persistence was paying off at last. Milo had never given up on his dreams—and now they were about to come true!